THE BIG PETS

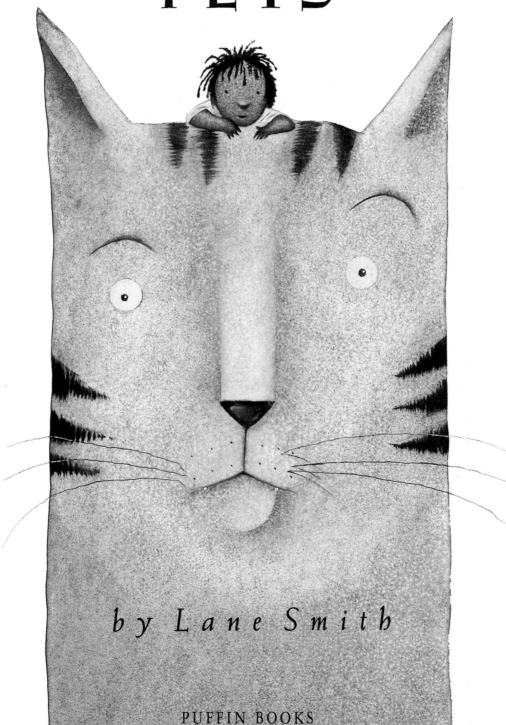

by Lane Smith

PUFFIN BOOKS

PUFFIN BOOKS
Published by the Penguin Group
Penguin Books USA Inc., 375 Hudson Street, New York, New York 10014, U.S.A.
Penguin Books Ltd, 27 Wrights Lane, London W8 5TZ, England
Penguin Books Australia Ltd, Ringwood, Victoria, Australia
Penguin Books Canada Ltd, 10 Alcorn Avenue, Toronto, Ontario, Canada M4V 3B2
Penguin Books (N.Z.) Ltd, 182–190 Wairau Road, Auckland 10, New Zealand

Penguin Books Ltd, Registered Offices: Harmondsworth, Middlesex, England

First published in the United States of America by Viking Penguin,
a division of Penguin Books USA Inc., 1991
Published in Puffin Books, 1993

1 3 5 7 9 10 8 6 4 2

LIBRARY OF CONGRESS CATALOGING-IN-PUBLICATION DATA
Smith, Lane.
The big pets / by Lane Smith.   p.   cm.
"First published in the United States of America by Viking Penguin . . . 1991" — T.p. verso.,
Summary: A little girl explores the mysterious dreamworld where small
children play with their big pets, which range from cats and
dogs to snakes and crickets.
ISBN 0-14-054265-5
[1. Animals—Fiction. 2. Pets—Fiction. 3. Dreams—Fiction.]   I. Title.
[PZ7.S6538Bi   1993]   [E]—dc20   93-18608   CIP   AC

Printed in Japan   Set in Weiss

To Sarah, Amy and Kyle
—L.S.

The girl was small and the cat was big.

And on certain nights
she rode on his back
to the place where
the Milk-Pool was.

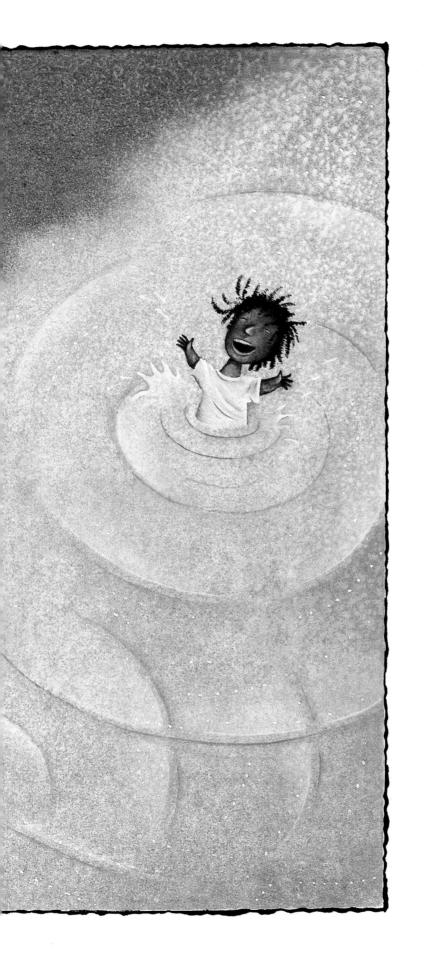

While he drank,
she swam.
And she came out
smelling like
fresh milk.

So did the other night children who gathered there.

The big cat would lick off the extra, then he and the girl
walked about, drying her hair in the warm night breeze.

Sometimes they saw
the small boy
who rode on the back
of the big dog.
And they waved
as he headed
for the Bone Gardens.

There, he played while his dog gnawed.

Together, they dug up old bones with
other kids who came with their dogs.

A mile away
at the Grassy Plains,
a dozen kids,
sometimes more,
rolled and tumbled
with their pet snakes.

And a little
beyond that,
children played
at the Hamster Holes.

And at Cricket Creek one little boy sat with his pet.

The cat and the girl often wondered what fun there was in that. Especially, when one could easily wish for a Milk-Pool...

or a Scratching Forest...

or a place where the
Stringy Vines teased.

And if one were truly
lucky, perhaps even...

...AN ENTIRE MILKY WAY.

The girl was small

and the cat was big.

And their nights always ended in the sleeping basket
that was just big enough for both of them.